I0749204

THE CAP OF INVISIBILITY

TAHIR SHAH

MARIETA KABADZHOVA

THE CAP OF INVISIBILITY

TAHIR SHAH

MARIETA KABADZHOVA

MMXXIII

Secretum Mundi Publishing Ltd
124 City Road
London
EC1V 2NX
United Kingdom

www.secretum-mundi.com
info@secretum-mundi.com

First published by Secretum Mundi Publishing Ltd in
Daydreams of an Octopus & Other Stories, 2022
Published in this edition, 2023

THE CAP OF INVISIBILITY

Artwork drawn by Marieta Kabadzhova

A CIP catalogue record for this title is available from the British Library.

VERSION 21112022

Visit the author's website:
Tahirshah.com

ISBN 978-1-914960-92-5

Once upon a time, a woman named Fatima was spinning wool in her cottage on the edge of the forest when a spider descended from the rafters and climbed over the yarn.

Noticing the arachnid, Fatima brushed at it.

As her fingers touched it, the spider swung away on a silken thread and was soon back in the shadows. Tut-tutting to herself, Fatima ran a hand up and down the yarn, hoping to clear away any trace of a web.

What the spinner had not comprehended
was that, rather than brushing the silk away
from the wool, she was in actual fact
brushing it into the yarn.

Without giving it any thought, she carried on with her spinning and, by the end of the afternoon, she had enough wool prepared to knit her husband the cap he had been asking for.

Next morning, Fatima made breakfast
for her children and bustled them
out of the house for school.

Once silence prevailed, she went over to her chair and picked up the balls of wool she had spun the day before.

But, to her unease, the yarn was
glistening in spider silk.

Cursing herself for not keeping
the house spick and span, she
once again brushed the silk away.

At least, that is what she
thought she was doing.

In actual fact, she was again brushing the fine gossamer of spider silk into the wool.

With the wind whipping through the trees outside, Fatima got down to knitting.

Within an hour or two, she had almost finished the cap. Holding it up to the light, she admired the colours and the shape, imagining how pleased her husband would be when he came home from chopping wood in the forest.

Late that afternoon, the children trooped in from school. The youngest, a little boy named Hashim, raced over to the knitting and when no one else was looking, he pulled on the cap.

At the very same moment, the cat upset a pan of milk on the stove. Fatima rushed to the kitchen, shooed away the animal, and got down to mop up the spill.

Then, when order reigned once again, she called her children around and explained that they would all surprise their father with the fine new cap she had knitted.

‘But where is the cap, Mother?’
asked Leila, the oldest child.
‘It’s there, on my chair.’
‘Where?’

Fatima became flustered, wondering if the cat had dragged it onto the floor. ‘That doesn’t make sense,’ she said.

'And where's little Hashim?'
asked the second daughter.

Clasping her hands to her cheeks,
Fatima called out for the youngest one.
'Are you sure he came home from
school with you all, my dears?'

'Yes, Mother!' the two daughters
exclaimed as one.
'Well, where could he have got to?'

Leila pointed to the chair, where a single ball of wool was sitting on the cushion.

'I saw him running over there, to—'
'To put on your father's new woollen cap!' Fatima broke in.

Just then, a shrill giggle was heard coming from behind the divan.

'Hashim?! Are you hiding there, you little rascal?!' the boy's mother cried. 'Come out at once!'

‘But I am here,’ Hashim said.
‘Well, if you’re there, why can’t we see you?’
snapped Leila.

‘And where’s the new woollen
cap I’ve just knitted for your father?’
Tugging it off his head, Hashim
held it out at arm’s length.

Instantly, he was visible,
standing before the others.

As her daughters looked on in
consternation, their mother exclaimed:
'What work of a jinn is this?!'

Shaking, Leila shared her fear,
that her little brother was possessed.

Fatima reached forward. In a single movement
she grabbed her little son, giving him the
strongest hug, as though they had been
apart for a lifetime and a half.

Her mind working at making sense of what had occurred, Fatima spoke:

'My grandmother once told me,' she said in less than a whisper, 'of a kind of spider that wove a special web.'

'What kind of web, Mother?'

'A web of invisibility. Anything it touched would be rendered unseen...'

As Fatima gave voice to her fear, she took the cap from little Hashim's hand and pulled it down over her own head.

Instantly, she vanished.

Within a minute or two, Fatima and each of her children had tried on the cap.

The youngest of the daughters was pulling the object from her head when the father of the house came home. He asked to know the reason for such high excitement.

'A miracle, Baba!' Leila cried.
'Miracle?! What miracle?!'
'A magic cap… the one Mother
has knitted for you.'

Speaking all at once, the children described what had happened. And when they were silent, Fatima gave her own explanation about the spider of which her grandmother had spoken.

The woodcutter's daughters were jumping
up and down, each of them begging to
have another chance to experience
the cap of invisibility.

Clapping his hands together in anger, their father ordered them to quieten down. 'Leila!' the woodcutter growled. 'You are to take that cap to the river and throw it in!'

Fearful at igniting their father's rage,
the children agreed.

‘Do as your father bids you when you have
done your homework, children,’
their mother said.

'But Mother, I don't have any homework tonight,' Leila answered. 'So I will take the cap down to the river and throw it in.'

Taking the cap in her hand, Leila went out of the house and made her way to the river.

As she strode through the forest, she turned the situation around in her mind.

‘If I do as my father says,’ she thought to herself, ‘the magic of the cap of invisibility will be lost. And if that happens, it cannot be used in times of need.

‘Although there’s no way to know what may happen to us in the future, it’s surely sensible to hide the cap of invisibility, so that it’s available.’

Leila was an obedient girl but, in her eyes, good sense outweighed obedience.

Accordingly, she wrapped the cap in her shawl, and stuffed it in a hollow in a blasted mulberry tree in the forest. Telling no one what she had done, she returned home.

To her surprise, neither of her parents, nor her siblings, mentioned the magic cap of invisibility again.

Days, weeks, and months passed.
Then half a year.

Leila forgot about hiding the magic cap, and it was as though the curious episode had never taken place.

One afternoon, while chopping wood, her father discovered a hoard of ancient gold coins hidden at the base of a tree he was cutting down.

He was sitting on the ground, hands filled with glinting coins, when a pair of soldiers from the royal guard approached.

Honest to the core, the woodcutter showed the coins to the soldiers and explained that he had just found them.

Certain no one would be so honest as to admit finding the coins, the soldiers assumed the woodcutter was only showing them a small fraction of a far larger treasure.

Drawing their swords, they threatened him. 'Reveal the entire hoard you have found, you wretched man,' one of them cried out, 'or we shall have you imprisoned in the deepest dungeon!'

Begging them to believe him, the woodcutter invited the soldiers to take what he had found.

‘I promise that I found no more of these,’ he insisted. ‘I am a simple man. And, although a treasure such as this would make a great difference to my existence, it is not my money to take.’

Making good on their threats, the officers of the royal guard put the woodcutter in chains and dragged him off to the dungeons.

Days passed before word of what had happened reached the ears of the woodcutter's family.

Distraught at the thought of her husband languishing in a cell, Fatima gathered her children around her and told them to have faith in the divine.

That night, all three children
and their mother prayed for
their father, and went to bed.
But Leila was unable to sleep.

Lying on her back, she kept thinking that there must be a way to save her beloved father from the terrible cell in which he was imprisoned.

As she lay there,
she remembered the magic cap.

When she was sure all the others were fast asleep, Leila crept out of the house, paced through the forest, and made her way to the blasted mulberry tree.

To her delight, the magic cap was still there, wrapped in her shawl, where she had left it months before.

Taking a deep breath, Leila pulled it on. She didn't feel any different, and wondered whether it had lost its ability to make things invisible. But, putting her hand in front of her face in the moonlight, she couldn't see it. She was even invisible to herself.

With no plan to speak of, she hurried through the forest and then through the town, until she arrived at the palace walls.

By this time, it was the middle of the night, and the streets were deserted.

A pair of low-ranking conscripts were standing guard at the gateway. Assuming they were alone, they were busily chatting to one another, telling jokes of the wise fool, Mulla Nasrudin.

Moving as fast as her feet could carry her, Leila hurried into the palace through a gap in the railings. She was going to try and locate the dungeons when something occurred to her…

…if she was to free her father,
the entire family would be rounded up,
and he himself would become a fugitive.

So, cautioning herself to think of a plan, she wandered the palace corridors, taking in the lavish surroundings.

Without meaning to trespass,
she found herself in the queen's
private chamber.

The walls were hung with the finest textiles from the Orient, and the floors were laid in exquisite teak with jewels inset.

In any other circumstances, Leila would have been more interested in the lavish décor, but all that was in her mind was saving her father.

Gliding in silence through the private apartment, the cap of invisibility pulled down tight, she heard the sound of a woman crying.

Unable not to be intrigued, Leila paced through to a bedroom from where the sound was coming.

Before she knew it, she was standing in
front of a grand bed, upon which
the queen was sitting.
Head in hands, she was sobbing.

Being naturally curious, Leila whispered:
'Dearest Queen, why do you weep?'

Startled at the sound of a child's voice,
the queen looked up.
'Who's there?!'

‘I am a good jinn,’ Leila said. ‘A good jinn who cares for your well-being.’

‘But your voice is that of a child,’
the queen said.
‘We jinn can take any form, as you know,’
said Leila.

The queen nodded.
'I have heard as much. But pray tell,
what can you do for me?'
'I will have to hear your predicament
in full before I can give help,' advised Leila.

A moment later, the queen was mid-flow in a story of trial, tribulation, and woe. The tale explained why she was sobbing on the edge of her bed in the middle of the night.

Despite endless twists, turns, and all manner of complexities, her misery came down to a single fact… that she had been robbed a year before while out riding.

While she was resting at the river's edge,
a golden brooch had been stolen from her
saddlebag by a fisherman.

She had learned of the theft from the kingdom's network of spies. Being a good queen, she didn't want to incriminate the fisherman.

But day after day, the king asked what
she had done with the golden brooch.

Once Leila had heard the tale,
she thought long and hard. And as first
light broke across the horizon, she said:

'In order to regain the brooch, you will need to arrange for a humble woodcutter to be released from the prison beneath this very palace, to be pardoned, and to be given the golden hoard he himself discovered.

'You will order him to go to the home of the fisherman and ask for the brooch. In return, the value of the brooch will be paid to the fisherman from the gold coins. Even though he had stolen, he will be thanked by the woodcutter for cooperating.'

‘And what do you require from me, O jinn?’

Leila thought for a moment.
'As a selfless jinn, I need nothing for myself,' she said. 'Instead, I ask that once each year, the wives and children of all woodcutters be honoured in a banquet here at the palace.'

The queen nodded.
It being the nod of royalty,
it was as good as any promise.

Before the sun had set on the kingdom, the woodcutter was released from the dungeons.

Dressed in fine attire and presented with the golden hoard he had discovered, he was sent to the home of the fisherman.

Once an appropriate explanation had been made, the fisherman was given the correct number of coins in exchange for the brooch, and that object was presented by the woodcutter to the hand of the queen.

Returned to his family, the woodcutter had no clear understanding of what had taken place.

Leila never explained her role in his release to anyone – not even when she, her siblings, and her mother were guests of honour at the annual banquet, as they always were.

As for the magic cap of invisibility, once the golden brooch had been returned and her father pardoned, Leila wrapped it back in her shawl, and took it back to the hollow in the blasted mulberry tree…

…where it is waiting for you to find it
and set out with it on a new adventure.

Finis

About the Author

Descended from a long line of storytellers, writers, and savants, Tahir Shah is one of the most prolific authors of his generation. He has published more than sixty books in numerous genres, including travel, fiction, and fantasy, as well as tales for children.

Raised in the tradition of Eastern 'teaching stories', Shah is passionate about stories and storytelling. He regards the ability to learn from folklore as being in us all, what he calls a 'default setting of humankind'. As well as having written scores of books, Shah has made documentaries for National Geographic TV and The History Channel. He is the founder and CEO of the charity, The Scheherazade Foundation.

About the Artist

Marieta Kabadzhova is a professional illustrator based in Bulgaria. For as long as she can remember, her two favourite things in the world have been drawing and reading. As an artist, Marieta strives to tell a story without words, experimenting with different techniques to allow the illustrations to come to life. She works with traditional mediums such as pen and ink, watercolour, and gouache, as well as creating digital artwork.

Books By Tahir Shah

Travel

Trail of Feathers
Travels With Myself
Beyond the Devil's Teeth
In Search of King Solomon's Mines
House of the Tiger King
In Arabian Nights
The Caliph's House
Sorcerer's Apprentice
Journey Through Namibia

Novels

Jinn Hunter: Book One – The Prism
Jinn Hunter: Book Two – The Jinnslayer
Jinn Hunter: Book Three – The Perplexity
Hannibal Fogg and the Supreme Secret of Man
Hannibal Fogg and the Codex Cartographica
Casablanca Blues
Eye Spy
Godman
Paris Syndrome
Timbuctoo

Nasrudin

Travels With Nasrudin
The Misadventures of the Mystifying Nasrudin
The Peregrinations of the Perplexing Nasrudin
The Voyages and Vicissitudes of Nasrudin
Nasrudin in the Land of Fools

Teaching Stories

The Arabian Nights Adventures

Scorpion Soup

Tales Told to a Melon

The Afghan Notebook

The Caravanserai Stories

Ghoul Brothers

Hourglass

Imaginist

Jinn's Treasure

Jinnlore

Mellified Man

Skeleton Island

Wellspring

When the Sun Forgot to Rise

Outrunning the Reaper

The Cap of Invisibility

On Backgammon Time

The Wondrous Seed

The Paradise Tree

Mouse House

The Hoopoe's Flight

The Old Wind

A Treasury of Tales

Daydreams of an Octopus & Other Stories

Miscellaneous

The Reason to Write

Zigzag Think

Being Myself

Research

Cultural Research

The Middle East Bedside Book

Three Essays

Anthologies

The Anthologies

The Clockmaker's Box

The Tahir Shah Fiction Reader

The Tahir Shah Travel Reader

Edited by

Congress With a Crocodile

A Son of a Son, Volume I

A Son of a Son, Volume II

Screenplays

Casablanca Blues: The Screenplay

Timbuctoo: The Screenplay

A REQUEST

If you enjoyed this book, please review it on your favourite online retailer or review website.

Reviews are an author's best friend.

To stay in touch with Tahir Shah, and to hear about his upcoming releases before anyone else, please sign up for his mailing list:

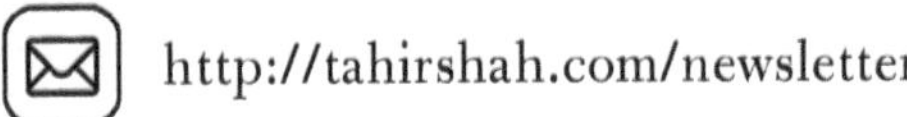

http://tahirshah.com/newsletter

And to follow him on social media, please go to any of the following links:

http://www.twitter.com/humanstew

@tahirshah999

http://www.facebook.com/TahirShahAuthor

http://www.youtube.com/user/tahirshah999

http://www.pinterest.com/tahirshah

https://www.goodreads.com/tahirshahauthor

http://www.tahirshah.com

www.ingramcontent.com/pod-product-compliance
Lightning Source LLC
Chambersburg PA
CBHW030522310726
48979CB00010B/1762/J

* 9 7 8 1 9 1 4 9 6 0 9 2 5 *